A Primary Source Guide to

INDIA

Autumn Leigh

The Rosen Publishing Group's

PowerKids Press™
PRIMARY SOURCE

New York

Published in 2003 by The Rosen Publishing Group, Inc.
29 East 21st Street, New York, NY 10010

Copyright © 2003 by The Rosen Publishing Group, Inc.

Book Design: Haley Wilson

Photo Credits: Cover, p. 1 © FPG International; p. 4 (map) © Map Resources; p. 4 (inset) © Jeremy Horner/ Corbis; p. 6 © David Samuel Robbins/Corbis; pp. 8, 10 © Bettmann/Corbis; p. 12 © John Noble/Corbis; p. 14 © Paul Harris/Stone; p. 16 © Archivo Iconografico, S.A./Corbis; p. 18 © Galen Rowell/Corbis; p. 20 © Brian A. Vikander/Corbis; p. 22 © EyeWire.

Library of Congress Cataloging-in-Publication Data

Leigh, Autumn.
  A primary source guide to India / Autumn Leigh.
      p. cm.
Summary: Text and photographs depict the history, government, culture, and traditions of India, which is about one-third the size of the United States but has about three times more people living there.
  ISBN: 0-8239-6596-1 (lib. bdg.)
  ISBN: 0-8239-8080-4 (pbk.)
  6-pack ISBN: 0-8239-8087-1
  1. India—Juvenile literature. [1. India.] I. Title.
  DS407 .R69 2003
  954—dc21

                                    2002004165

Manufactured in the United States of America

Contents

TURKMENISTAN

Hindu Kush

Ghazni

AFGHANISTAN

PAKISTAN

Naushahro Firoz

New Delhi ★

G r e a t

I n d i a n

D e s e r t

I N D I A

CHINA

P l a t e a u

o f

T i b e t

Great Himalaya Range

NEPAL

BHUTAN

Ganges

Calcutta•

Arabian Sea

Bombay•
(Mumbai)

Western Ghats

Krishna R.

Eastern Ghats

Madras•

Bay

of

Bengal

SRI
LANKA

4

India

India is a country in South Asia. India is about one-third the size of the United States, but it has about three times as many people as the United States does. Only China has more people than India. Bombay—also called Mumbai—is the largest city in India. New Delhi is India's capital.

Much of India is hot and dry for most of the year. India has a "rainy season" between June and September. During this time, strong winds called monsoons bring large amounts of rain to India. Many Indian farmers depend on the monsoons to provide enough water for their crops.

◀ India's Ganges River is one of the longest rivers in the world. Many Indians believe the Ganges River is holy and has the power to wash away their sins.

The Land of the Subcontinent

India is a peninsula. A peninsula is an area of land surrounded by water on three sides. India has deserts, plains, beaches, rain forests, tall mountain ranges, and many rivers.

India was once separate from Asia. Millions of years ago, India, Australia, Antarctica, and other lands were a single giant continent. They slowly separated and drifted apart. India pushed against Asia, which made the land's edge rise high and become the Himalaya mountains. India is still drifting and pushing north. That is why the Himalayas are still "growing."

◄ The Himalayas are the highest mountains in the world. The tops of the mountains are covered with snow all year long. The word *Himalaya* means "House of Snow."

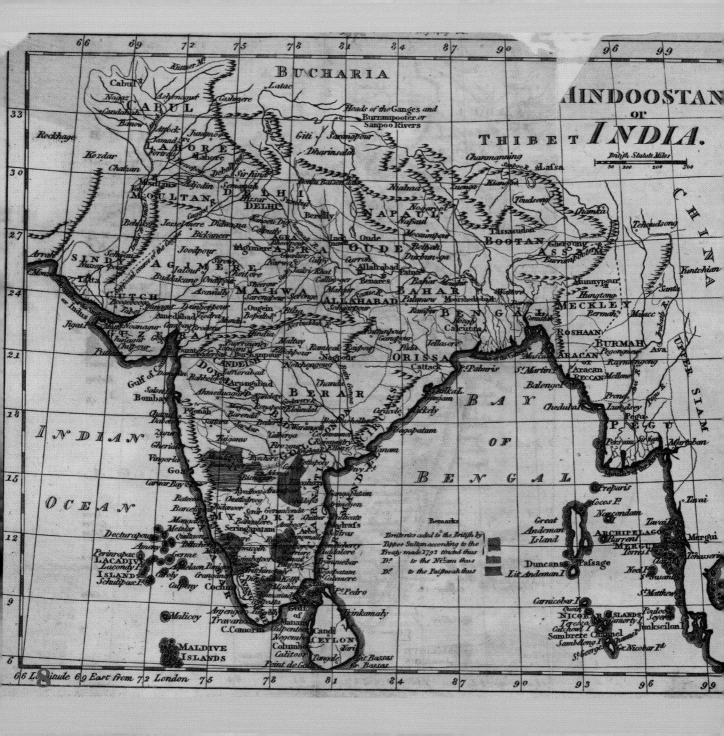

HINDOOSTAN or INDIA.

British Statute Miles

BUCHARIA

THIBET

CHINA

Heads of the Ganges and Burrampooter or Sanpoo Rivers

Cabul Tª

CABUL

Kozdar

Rockhage

Chatzan

Cashmere

LAHORE
Lahore

MOULTAN

DELHI
Delhi

Sirhind

NAPAUL
Napaul

BOOTAN

ASSAM

Lassa

Charannanning

MECKLEY

SINDY

AGIMERE

AGRA
OUDE

Allahabad
Benares

BAHAR

BENGAL
Calcutta

BURMAH

ARACAN
or
Aracan
RECCAN

Ava

UPPER SIAM

CUTCH

GUZERAT

Amedabad

Bombay

MALWA

ALLAHABAD

Nagpour

ORISSA
Cattack

Pt. Palmiras

St Martins

MASULIPATAM

CANDEISH

DOW

BERAR

CIRCARS

BAY

OF

BENGAL

PEGU

Pegue

Martaban

INDIAN

OCEAN

GOA
Goa

Carwar Bay

MYSORE
Bangalore
Seringapatam

Madras

Pondicherry

Chedubah

Preparis

Cocos I.

Nascondam

Great
Andeman
Island

Lit. Andeman I.

Duncans Passage

ARCHIPELAGO

MERGUI

Tavai

Decturapour

LACADIVE
ISLANDS

Cochin

Malicoy

MALDIVE
ISLANDS

C. Comorin

Travancore

CEYLON

Trinkomaly

Point de Galle

Gr. Bassas
or Bassas

Carnicobar I.

NICOBAR ISLANDS

Sombrero Channel

Gr. Nicobar Iª

St Matthew

Remarks

Territories ceded to the British by Tippoo Sultan according to the Treaty made 1792 tinted thus
Dº. to the Nizam thus
Dº. to the Paishwah thus

The History of India

One of the world's first great **civilizations** existed about 4,500 years ago along the Indus River in what is now western India and Pakistan. Its people had systems of writing, counting, and measuring.

By around 1500 A.D., European countries began trading with India. England took control of India in the mid-1700s and ruled the country for about 200 years. In 1947, India gained its independence from England.

◄ Mahatma Gandhi helped India win its freedom from England. Gandhi believed in protesting peacefully against things that were wrong. He is shown here on an Indian banknote.

◄ This map of India (also called "Hindoostan" in the upper right corner) was made around 1800, when England controlled India.

Indian Government

The nation of India is the largest federal republic, or **democracy**, in the world. The president is elected by **representatives** of the Indian people. The House of the People consists of 545 representatives, most of whom are elected by the people. The Council of States is made up of 250 members elected by other politicians from each state, including the president.

The president of India appoints a prime minister, who is the most powerful person in India's government. The prime minister, who is a member of the House of the People, runs the government on a day-to-day basis.

◀ After India gained its independence from England in 1947, Jawaharlal Nehru (left) became India's first prime minister. He worked hard to improve living conditions in India. Nehru's daughter, Indira Gandhi (right), became prime minister in 1966.

The Economy of India

Most of India's people are farmers. About half of India is made up of farmland. India's largest crop is rice. Only China produces more rice than India. Farmers also grow grains, tea, vegetables, **mangoes**, and spices. India has so many farms that it usually does not need to import food from other countries. However, many farmers are only able to grow enough food for their own families.

India has large mining and fishing industries. Companies in India make iron, steel, and cloth. They trade these things with other countries for oil and machinery.

◀ Almost two-thirds of India's workers make their living on farms. These people are picking tea at a plantation in the city of Darjeeling in western India.

The Caste System

Indian society was once strictly divided into social groups called castes. The **caste system** is part of **Hinduism**, a religion practiced throughout India. Priests and teachers made up the highest group. People called "untouchables" were considered too low to even belong to a caste and usually held jobs considered "dirty" by Hindus. People from different castes were not allowed to mix with each other.

Today, the caste system is not as important as it once was. It is now illegal to treat "untouchables" badly. However, some people still follow the old rules, especially in small towns and villages.

◄ There are twenty national languages in India, including Hindi, which is used widely. English is also spoken by many people who work in business and education.

[illegible]

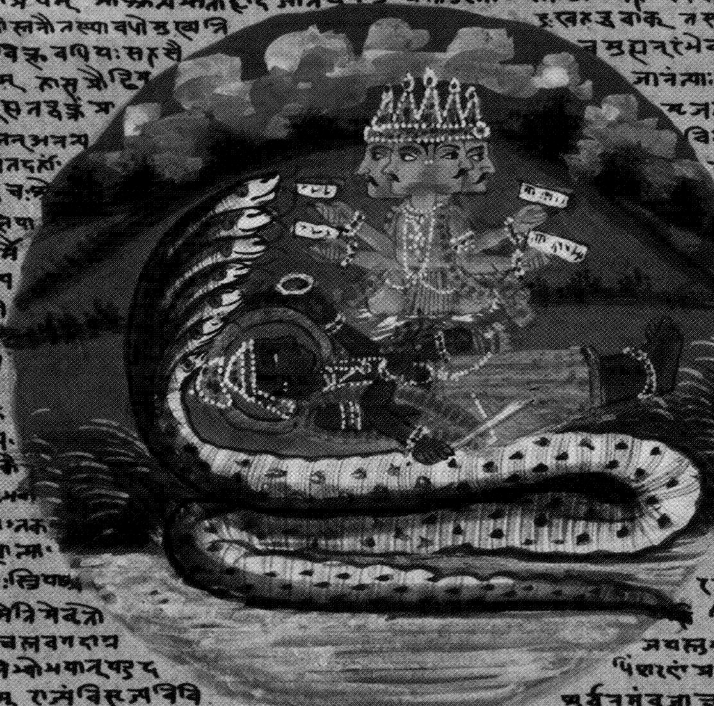

[illegible]

Hinduism

Most Indian people practice Hinduism. Hindus believe they will be reborn as another person or creature after they die. Whether their next life will be good or bad depends on how they treated others in their earlier lives. India also has one of the largest **Muslim** populations in the world.

Hindus have many festivals that mix religious **ceremonies** with parades, fireworks, and great feasts. One festival, called Diwali, celebrates the victory of a god over an evil demon. During Diwali, Hindus decorate their houses and the streets of their villages, towns, and cities with bright lights.

◄ This is part of a "Purana," a Hindu holy book that has stories about gods, goddesses, and heroes. Puranas contain Hindu beliefs about how the world was created. This copy was made in the 1700s in an ancient Indian language called Sanskrit. In the middle is a small painting of Hindu gods.

Art from Yesterday and Today

The Indian people have been creating beautiful buildings for more than 2,500 years. There are ancient Hindu temples all over India decorated with beautiful **statues** and stone carvings. Other Indian art forms include colorful paintings, music, dance, and religious writings dating back 3,000 years.

Today, films are a popular form of art in India. Many families enjoy gathering around the television at night or going out to the movies. Indian films are also popular in the Middle East, parts of Africa, and in the Caribbean.

◀ One of the most famous buildings in the world, the Taj Mahal, is found in northern India. A Muslim emperor named Shah Jahan had it built in the mid-1600s as a resting place for his dead wife, Mumtaz Mahal. It took about 20,000 people twenty-two years to build it!

Planning for the Future

Since India gained its freedom from England in 1947, the people's quality of life has improved greatly. India is now seen as a major world power. However, India faces overpopulation. Sickness, pollution, unclean water, and too little energy to support the growing population are becoming serious problems. India has disagreements with nearby China, Pakistan, and Bangladesh about borders and the sharing of water. The Indian people are working hard to solve these problems so their children can have a safe and bright future.

◀ Women from Rajasthan, in northern India, wear colorful clothes, which contrast with the sandy desert region they live in. They are attending the famous Pushkar Fair, an annual Hindu holiday.

India at a Glance

Population: About 1,030,000,000
Capital City: New Delhi (population about 300,000)
Largest City: Bombay (population about 12,000,000)
Official Name: Republic of India
National Anthem: "Jana-gana-mana"
("Thou Art the Ruler of the Minds of All People")
Land Area: 1,269,346 square miles (3,287,591 square kilometers)
Government: Federal republic
Unit of Money: Indian rupee
Flag: The flag of India has three stripes: yellowish-orange stands for courage, white stands for truth, and green stands for faith. In the middle is a Buddhist symbol, the Wheel of Law.

Glossary

caste system (KAST SIHS-tuhm) A system that separates people in a society into different levels. People in higher castes have more rights than people in lower castes.

ceremony (SAIR-uh-moh-nee) A special act or set of acts done for a special occasion, such as a holiday.

civilization (sih-vuh-luh-ZAY-shuhn) A way of life followed by the people of a certain time and place.

democracy (dih-MAH-kruh-see) A system of government that is run by the people it governs.

Hinduism (HIN-doo-ih-zuhm) A religion that teaches that people are reborn as other people or creatures after they die.

mango (MAN-goh) An oval fruit with orange or green skin, soft, sweet flesh, and a large pit.

Muslim (MUHZ-luhm) A person who practices the religion of Islam. Muslims believe in one god, Allah, and follow the teachings of Allah's messenger, Muhammad.

representative (reh-prih-ZEN-tuh-tihv) Someone who acts in place of others.

statue (STA-choo) A work of art that is shaped like a person, animal, or other figure.

Index

Primary Source List

Page 4 (inset). Woman bathing in Ganges River, Varanasi. Photograph taken by Jeremy Horner on April 12, 1996.

Page 8. *Hindoostan or India*. Engraved map by John Walker, 1798.

Page 9. 500-rupee banknote, with portrait of Mahatma Gandhi.

Page 10. Photograph of Jawaharal Nehru and his daughter, Indira Gandhi. Taken March 14, 1955, in New Delhi.

Page 16. Page from a copy of the Bhagavata Purana with miniature painting of Vishnu, Brahma, and Sesha Nag, 1700s.

Page 18. Taj Mahal, Agra, 1632–1654.

Page 20. Rajputs wearing veils and native dress at the Pushkar Fair. Photograph taken by Brian A. Vikander in November 1988 in Pushkar.

Web Sites

Due to the changing nature of Internet links, The Rosen Publishing Group, Inc. has developed an on-line list of Web sites related to the subjects of this book. This site is updated regularly. Please use this link to access the list:
http://www.powerkidslinks.com/pswc/psin/